Will You Help Me Fall Asleep?

Written by Anna Kang

Illustrated by Christopher Weyant

HARPER
An Imprint of HarperCollinsPublishers

I can't sleep!
I am
WIDE AWAKE!

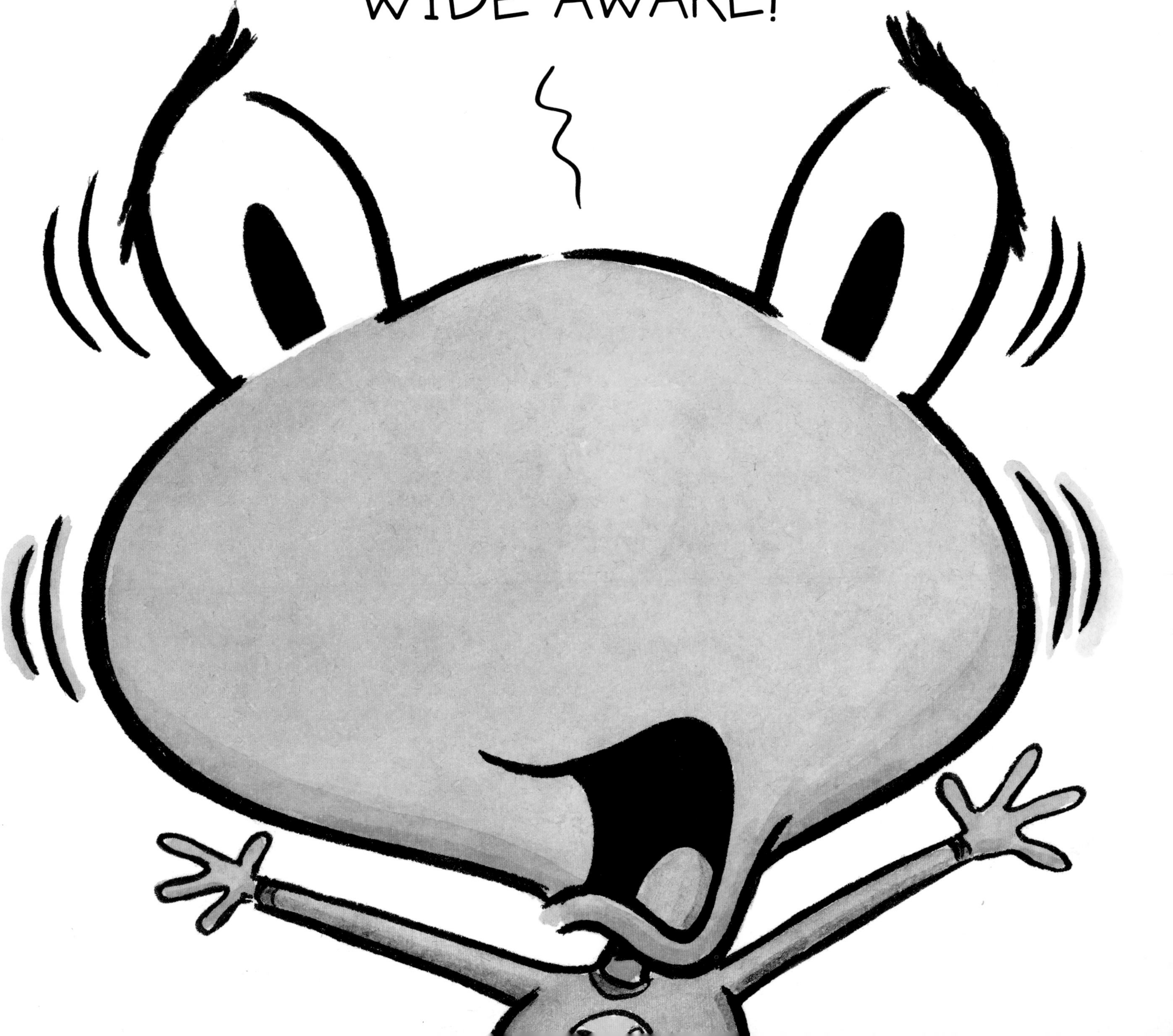

And do you know what else?
I'm going to be in big, big trouble.

And my mom *always* knows if I don't get a good night's sleep. I don't know how she knows, but she does.

I race my boat every year. All my friends will be there. I just *have* to go to the boat races!

What's that? Sleep?? I told you, I'm trying but I can't!

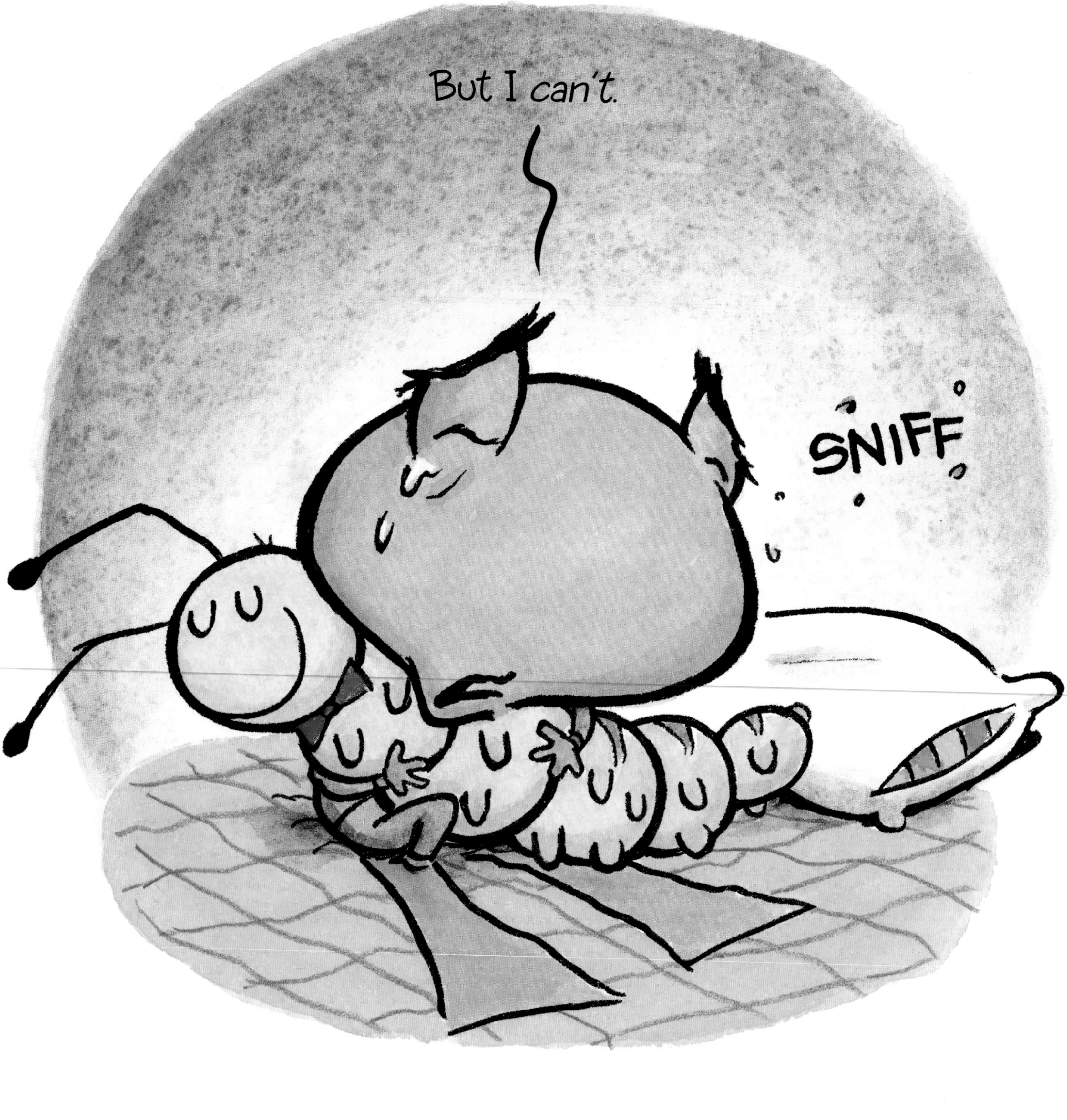
But I can't.
SNIFF

When I get sad at school Miss Chon tells me to take a slow, deep breath.

She says to go to my "happy place."

YAWN!

I love the boat races. . . .

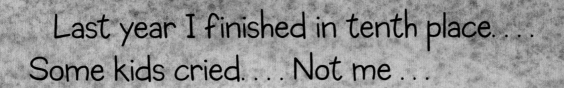

Last year I finished in tenth place. . . .
Some kids cried. . . . Not me . . .

I was happy. . . .

That was such a good day. . . .

Thanks for your help and for being . . . my . . . friend. . . .

To children everywhere, may you have sweet dreams.

With love, Anna & Chris

Will You Help Me Fall Asleep?
Text copyright © 2018 by Anna Kang
Illustrations copyright © 2018 by Christopher Weyant
All rights reserved. Manufactured in China.
No part of this book may be used or reproduced in any manner whatsoever
without written permission except in the case of brief quotations embodied in
critical articles and reviews. For information address HarperCollins Children's Books,
a division of HarperCollins Publishers, 195 Broadway, New York, NY 10007
www.harpercollinschildrens.com

ISBN 978-0-06-239685-3

The artist used watercolors and ink on 260 lb Arches paper to create the illustrations for this book.
18 19 20 21 22 SCP 10 9 8 7 6 5 4 3 2 1

❖

First Edition